Books by Marcus Pfister

THE RAINBOW FISH*
THE CHRISTMAS STAR*
DAZZLE THE DINOSAUR*
PENGUIN PETE
PENGUIN PETE'S NEW FRIENDS
PENGUIN PETE AND PAT
PENGUIN PETE, AHOY!
PENGUIN PETE AND LITTLE TIM
HOPPER
HOPPER HUNTS FOR SPRING
HOPPER'S EASTER SURPRISE
HANG ON, HOPPER!
CHRIS & CROC

*also available in Spanish

Copyright © 1995 by NordSüd Verlag AG, Zürich, Switzerland
First published in Switzerland under the title Der Regenbogenfisch hilft einen Fremdling
English translation copyright © 1995 by North-South Books Inc.
All rights reserved. No part of this book may be reproduced or utilized in any form
or by any means, electronic or mechanical, including photocopying,
recording, or any information storage and retrieval system,
without permission in writing from the publisher.

First published in the United States, Great Britain, Canada,
Australia, and New Zealand in 1995 by North-South Books Inc.,
an imprint of NordSüd Verlag AG, Zürich, Switzerland.
Distributed in the United States by North-South Books Inc., New York.

Library of Congress Cataloging-in-Publication Data is available.
A CIP catalogue record for this book is available from The British Library.
ISBN-13: 978-3-314-01574-8 / ISBN-10: 3-314-01574-7 (Paperback)
1 3 5 7 9 PB 10 8 6 4 2
Printed in Belgium

MARCUS PFISTER

RAINBOW FISH TO THE RESCUE!

TRANSLATED BY J. ALISON JAMES

NORTHSOUTH
BOOKS

A long way out in the deep blue sea
there swam a school of fish. Not just ordinary
fish—each one had a sparkling silver scale.
Ever since Rainbow Fish had shared his scales,
these fish had done everything together.
They swam together. They played together.
They ate together. They even rested together,
floating in the shadows of the reef.

They were so happy together, they had
no interest in other fish. So one day, when
a little striped fish swam through their game
of flash-tag, they all stared at him.

"Hey," the little striped fish finally said,
"Can I play too?"

"It's flash-tag," said one little fish, "and
you don't have a flashing scale!"

"Do you have to have a special scale?" the little striped fish asked.

"Of course you do!" said the fish with the jagged fins. "Come on, let's play!" he called to the others. "Don't worry about him."

Then all the fish turned and went back to their game.

Rainbow Fish hesitated. He was afraid of losing his new friends, so he didn't dare stand up to the fish with the jagged fins. Feeling a little ashamed, Rainbow Fish reluctantly swam off to join the others.

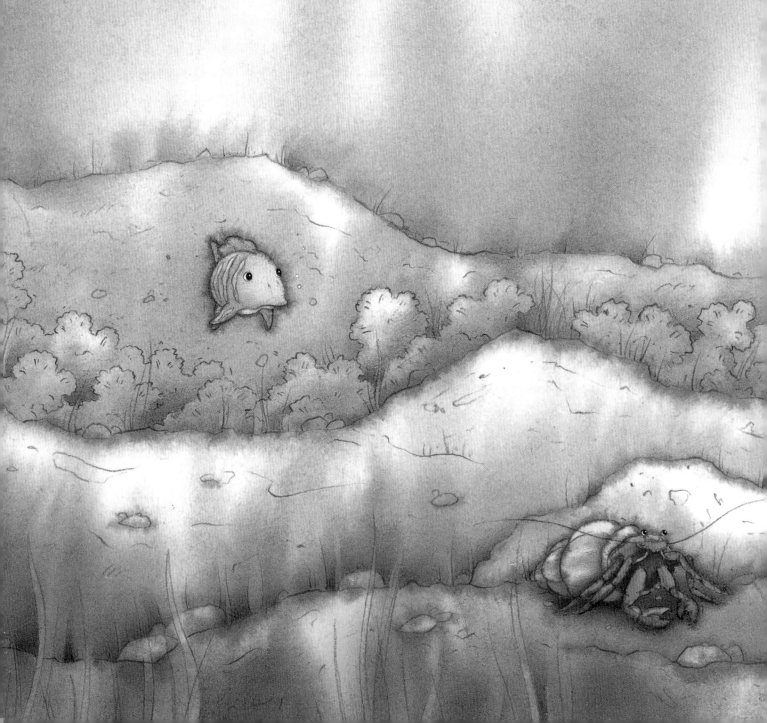

The little striped fish floated all alone at the edge of the reef. He looked sad as he watched the game. The other fish were having such fun—darting and diving in the deep blue sea, their shiny scales sparkling.

Rainbow Fish remembered what it felt like to have no friends and how lonely he had been when all the fish had ignored him. He had been so proud of all his glittering scales that he had refused to share them. No wonder nobody had wanted to play with him.

But now his friends did want him to play, and Rainbow Fish soon was caught up in the game.

No one was paying attention when danger entered the reef. . . .

Suddenly a shark shot like an arrow into the middle of the school. The fish darted in every direction and managed to escape to their hiding place.

There, in a narrow crack in the reef, the shark could not reach them. They were safe.

But the little striped fish wasn't. Rainbow Fish couldn't keep still, he was so worried.

"What's wrong?" asked the skinny fish.

"It's the little striped fish," said Rainbow Fish. "He's all alone out there. We've got to help him!"

With that, Rainbow Fish left the safety of
the hiding place. "Let's go!" he called.
　　The other fish trembled with fear, but they
knew what they had to do. They sped out
of the crack after Rainbow Fish.

They soon saw the shark. And there was the little
striped fish, swimming and spinning away from his jaws.
Rainbow Fish could see that the little fish's strength was
failing fast.

"Hurry!" shouted Rainbow Fish, and all the fish
swarmed straight for the shark. This confused the shark,
because usually fish swam away from him. He turned this
way and that, snapping right and left until he was dizzy.
The shark almost got the fish with the jagged fins, but he
escaped with just a few scratches.

Quietly, Rainbow Fish led the little striped fish to safety.

"You were really brave," said the little striped fish. "Thanks for saving my life."

Together, they watched as the exhausted shark gave up and swam away.

When all the fish returned safely to the reef, they welcomed the little striped fish.

"Why don't you stay and play with us?" Rainbow Fish offered.

"How can I play flash-tag when I don't have a shiny scale?" asked the little striped fish.

"We can play fin-tag instead!" said the fish with the jagged fin. "Touch a fin and you're it!"

All the fish cheered, and then they swam off to play together in the deep blue sea.